Vici Molloy is a mother of two boys who lives in Surrey. She has spent most of her adult life working in childcare, primarily as a nanny. Vici has always had a passion for poetry and of course reading. Her stories are based on her own experiences from her childhood as well as her life as a mummy and her many years as a professional nanny.

SLEEPY RABBITY

Vici Molloy

AUSTIN MACAULEY PUBLISHERS™
LONDON • CAMBRIDGE • NEW YORK • SHARJAH

A CIP catalogue record for this title is available from the British Library.

ISBN 9781398456334 (Paperback)
ISBN 9781398456341 (Hardback)
ISBN 9781398456358 (ePub e-book)

www.austinmacauley.com

First Published 2023
Austin Macauley Publishers Ltd®
25 Canada Square
Canary Wharf
London
E14 5LQ

Dedicated to my boys, George and Matthew. You are my inspiration and I love you with all my heart.

I have many people to thank for their support and belief in me. Candice, my unofficial proofreader and biggest cheerleader, always giving me the nudge I needed exactly when I needed it. Gemma, my market research, who gave me the most amazing and detailed feedback and therefore the courage to submit my work. My husband Dave for keeping me grounded throughout and my wonderful parents, Maria and Tim, who have supported me and believed in me from the very beginning until this very day. Thank you all so much.

Come on, Rabbity, sleepy head,
it's time I took you up to bed.

Let's wash your face and brush your teeth.

Or two or three?
The stars are out, the moon is bright, it's time
for Rabbity to say goodnight.

but I can't sleep just yet dear mummy,
my mouth is dry and I have a sore tummy.

We've brushed your teeth in perfect time, you've had a drink, your tummy is fine.

The stars are out, the moon is bright, it's time for Rabbity to say goodnight.

But, Mummy, my blanket's making me grumpy,

because it's not on right and my pillow's all lumpy.

The blanket's pulled 'round you nice and tight, you've fluffed your pillow, so it feels just right.

The stars are out, the moon is bright, it's time for Rabbity to say goodnight.

Can we have one more story, please?
And put the lamp on, so I can see?

We've read a story and turned out the light,
you mustn't fuss and you mustn't fight.

The stars are out, the moon is bright, it's
time for Rabbity to say goodnight.

But, Mummy, no, I can't go to bed,
I need to find my favourite ted!

15

I see your teddy, it's by your side. You haven't lost him, he didn't hide.

The stars are out, the moon is bright, it's time for Rabbity to say goodnight.

But, Mummy,
I've missed one thing off my list...

I need to give you a hug and a kiss!

Oh yes, you do, my little love, you
need to give me your biggest hug,
and we need to have a nice big kiss,
that is something we cannot miss.

I love you so much, with all my might, so have
sweet dreams, my love. Sleep tight.
The stars are out, the moon is bright, it's time
for Rabbity to say..."